For Aunt Viv and Uncle
Murray, whose kindness
knows no bounds

ORCHARD BOOKS

First published in 2015 in the United States by Little, Brown and Company
This edition published in 2015 by The Watts Publishing Group

3 5 7 9 10 8 6 4

A CIP catalogue record for this book is available from the British Library.

ISBN 978 1 40833 702 8

Printed and bound in Great Britain by CPI Group (UK) Ltd, Croydon, CR0 4YY

MIX
Paper from
responsible sources
FSC® C104740
www.fsc.org

The paper and board used in this book are made from wood from responsible sources

Orchard Books
An imprint of Hachette Children's Group
Part of The Watts Publishing Group Limited
Carmelite House, 50 Victoria Embankment, London EC4Y 0DZ

An Hachette UK Company
www.hachette.co.uk
www.hachettechildrens.co.uk

Fluttershy

✶ ✶ and ✶ ✶
The Furry
Friends Fair

Written by G. M. Berrow

ORCHARD

Contents

☆ ☆ ☆

Chapter 1

The Top Hat Bunny Cabaret

The local park was a haven of peaceful
relaxation for the residents of Ponyville.
The leafy trees and little hills covered in
soft green grass were perfect for
stretching out one's wings, reading a
book, or just looking at the clouds above
and daydreaming about what shapes the

Pegasi in Cloudsdale might make next.

A sweet yellow Pegasus pony named Fluttershy lived on the outskirts of town and loved to trot through the park every single day. It was nice to take a break from her busy job as a caretaker of animals, big and small. When she went on her walks, Fluttershy liked to reflect on her life and think about how lucky she was that it was one filled with fun, furry creatures and friends.

One day, as she strolled along on her normal route, Fluttershy noticed that something was different about Ponyville Park. There was a jaunty melody echoing across the grass, through the hedges, over the hills, and under the shade of the tall oaks. It sounded like it was coming from the area near Froggy Bottom Bogg. Though Fluttershy had every intention of ignoring the distraction, her pet bunny, Angel, went hopping towards the noise.

"Oh, OK, Angel," whispered the meek yellow Pegasus. Angel Bunny had Fluttershy wrapped around his furry little paw. It was hard for her to say no to such an adorable face.

"Let's go see what that commotion is, you curious little dear." Fluttershy brushed her soft pink mane away from her left eye, spread her wings, and flew after him. "I'm sure it won't take too long."

In truth, Fluttershy *actually* wanted to go home for a cup of dandelion tea and a nap with her new litter of kittens, but she wasn't going to ruin Angel's fun. He was only a young bunny and needed plenty of new experiences to grow – in addition to healthy food and weekly tail fluffings. Fluttershy had noticed that lately Angel had been very curious about all the 'hoppenings' in Ponyville. Just today, Fluttershy had taken him to the Ponyville Schoolhouse to visit the fillies and colts during break time. Then they'd gone to the market to see if there were any cherries for sale, and finally to Sugarcube Corner for a special bunny carrot cupcake made by Pinkie Pie. A busy day by anybunny's standards.

Angel arched his head back to marvel

 at the sight. The tent in front of them was huge, with red and white vertical stripes.

What's this, Fluttershy? Angel Bunny's big eyes said.

Fluttershy had a special connection with all her animals. She almost always knew exactly what they were trying to say, whether they could use their voices to tell her or not. Angel was particularly unique, though. Fluttershy could look into his eyes and know exactly what he was trying to tell her. Most of the time, anyway. Sometimes it took a few guesses.

"I'm not sure what's inside, Angel, but I think I've seen it before..." Fluttershy replied. The tent was definitely familiar. The triangular yellow flags at the top had the symbol of two hats side by side. Fluttershy scrunched up her nose in polite distaste. It was those swindlers the Flim Flam brothers again! They weren't very nice ponies.

"We don't want to go in there," Fluttershy said, looking down at Angel.

Flim and Flam had made a business out of creating fake get-well tonics and rotten apple juice. They were always looking for the next cheap way to make money from unsuspecting ponies.

I want to see! Angel hopped up and down excitedly and forged ahead to get a closer look at the two framed posters near the entrance.

Farnum and Failey present the Top Hat Bunny Cabaret

they said in big, bubbly letters. A picture of a brown rabbit with very long fur was in the middle. He was wearing a red bow tie and sitting on a black top hat. There was a flag in his paw that said,

Featuring the most talented bunnies in Equestria (plus frogs). Rabbits & Ribbits!

Angel pointed his paw at the poster and smiled. *Can we go inside?*

"Well, that's not what I was expecting at all." Fluttershy giggled. "I suppose if anything can get my attention, it's cute bunnies." Angel turned to her and crossed his arms with a pout. Suddenly, he didn't like the idea of Fluttershy paying more attention to other bunnies than to him. "Don't worry, little love. You're *my* top bunny!" Fluttershy patted Angel on his downy head and purchased two tickets for the show.

CHAPTER 2

Just a Frog and Bunny Show

Inside the tent, there was a flurry of preshow activity. Ponies were taking their seats on the wooden stands, buying refreshments to munch on (the popcorn came in a cardboard top hat), and chatting about what sorts of amazing bunny tricks they were about to behold. Fluttershy had never seen so many ponies excited about bunnies in one place. She was in great company.

Angel led the way to the front row and took a seat right in the middle. He clearly didn't want to miss a single hop or nose twitch of the performance.

"Do you want some carrot juice, Angel?" Fluttershy asked, gesturing to the refreshment stand. She always tried to make sure her pets stayed hydrated.

The little white rabbit shook his head and pointed to the seat next to him.

"Not even just a sip or two?" Fluttershy replied hopefully.

Angel stuck his nose in the air and pointed to the seat again. Fluttershy sat down. What a convincing fellow he was!

As the rest of the audience found their seats, Fluttershy petted Angel's soft white ears and smiled. This was a nice treat for the two of them. Maybe if the show was really entertaining, she would bring some of the birds and squirrels by tomorrow for a field trip. Or Toby the fruit bat. Toby *did* love a good cabaret.

The jaunty music began to play again, and a tiny marching band of bunnies entered the stage wearing blue costumes with sparkling gold buttons, each playing a different instrument. Leading the way was a large black rabbit with white spots playing a tuba. *Honk, honk. Honk, honk.* The bunnies hopped into formation, and a moment later, two tall yellow stallions danced onstage. They had short red manes and wore black tuxedos and top hats. One of them had a red moustache.

"I'm Farnuuuum!" sang Flim, extending a hoof out to the right.

"And I'm Faaaailey!" added Flam, reaching his hoof out to the left.

"Welcome to the Top Hat Bunny Cabaret – exciting entertainment every day!" They danced around each other in time to the music. "We bet you've never laid your EYES, on bunnies like these little GUYS!"

"You're in for a treat!" Flim shouted.

"You're in for a PRIZE!" Flam warbled. "The Top Hat Bunny Cabaret! Ponies, what d'ya saaay?!" Flam put his hoof to his ear as if he were listening.

"OK!" the ponies in the crowd shouted.

"Hooray!" shouted Flim in response.

"Because we've got Fuzzy Lops and Himalayans, Hot-de-Trots – know what we're sayin'?" Flim and Flam turned to the bunnies and patted each one on the head as they sang, *"Golden Palomino or Harlequin, whichever you like – we're not fussy!"*

Flam took off his top hat, waved a wand around and then pulled out a light purple rabbit wearing sunglasses. The rabbit began to juggle three golden orbs while hopping on one foot. The audience clapped and cheered. "See? This one can juggle balls!"

"That one can hop up walls!" Flim shouted, pointing to a long-haired grey bunny hopping sideways up the wall of the tent.

"This one cooks macaroni!" A tiny spotted bunny stirred a bubbling pot and

 waved to the crowd. He sprinkled some cheese on the pasta and scooped up a serving for a mint-green pony named Lyra. Lyra smiled and began to gobble up the yummy food.

"That one can lift a pony!" Sure enough, a little white bunny with black ears hopped over to Sea Swirl and lifted the pony high into the air. It was unbelievable!

Meanwhile, the frogs and bunnies in the band continued to play their instruments, dancing back and forth to the lyrics. On every fourth beat, the frogs would croak. Flim and Flam did a spin in time with each other and reached their hooves to the crowd.

"So get ready to feast your EYES, on these amazing little GUYS!"

"The unsurpassable!"

"...most desirable!"

"So incredible!"

"...try *commendable*!"

Flim and Flam shuffled to the sides of the stage and held their hooves out to present the bunnies. "The *hippity-hoppity*! Ribbity-rabbity! Tippity-toppity...Top Hat Bunny Cabareeeeeeet!"

"Plus frogs!" croaked Flam.

"Croaaak," said a toad.

The audience erupted in excited cheers, stomping their hooves on the ground in grand applause. Angel got up from his seat and began to hop up and down, clasping his paws together. His eyes sparkled with

wonder, and a big smile was plastered on his face. Fluttershy felt all warm and fuzzy inside at his elation. There was nothing better than seeing one of her pets happy.

CHAPTER 3

A Little Bunny of Little Talent

"That *was* a good show, wasn't it, Angel?" Fluttershy patted him on the head and stood up. She stomped her hooves on the ground a few times to show her appreciation, then trotted toward the exit. "Come along, sweetie. We have to get home for dinner."

Fluttershy was almost at the door when she turned around to ask Angel if he wanted a cucumber and lettuce sandwich or a salad of carrots. But the bunny wasn't there. Fluttershy scanned the room, only slightly panicked. He couldn't have hopped too far away in just a minute... could he?

A small crowd of ponies was gathered around something in the corner. Perhaps one of them had seen which way Angel had gone. "Excuse me?" Fluttershy whispered, tapping the shoulder of a blue Unicorn. The mare didn't budge. "Oh, um... hello?" she tried a little bit louder. "Have you seen my bunny?"

Fluttershy's question was interrupted by the distinct laughter of Flim coming from the middle of the group. Fluttershy tried to push her way through the crowd to get a better look at what was going on, but she didn't want to push too hard and bother anypony. She spread her wings and drifted up to hover above them.

In the middle of the circle was none other than Angel Bunny!

"Angel!" Fluttershy squeaked in shock and flew down to her pet, putting a protective hoof around him. "I'm really sorry. He's a little bit dehydrated and hasn't had his dinner yet—"

"Not at all, miss," Flim exclaimed, tipping his hat. "He was just trying to tell us something." He turned to the crowd and added, "Just another example of how great Farnum and Failey are with *all* bunnies, folks!"

"It seemed important!" added Flam, kneeling down on his forelegs. "Go on, little fellow."

Angel rolled his eyes and pointed to the Himalayan rabbit who had been playing the drums, then back to himself.

"You like his costume?" Fluttershy asked, cocking her head to the side.

Angel shook his head. He did a small cartwheel.

"I think this little fellow wants to join the show!" shouted Flim. "Brother, what d'ya say? Could we use this average-looking bunny in our extravaganza?"

Flam rubbed his mustache and trotted around Angel, sizing him up. "He does look a little bit plain … but we can work with that!" Flam pushed Fluttershy aside and leaned in close to Angel. "The real question is – what can he *do*?!"

"Can you do trapeze?" asked Flim.

"Can you ride on skis?" questioned Flam.

"Jump through a burning ring of fire?"

"Or perhaps hop on a greasy wire?"

At each suggestion, Angel shook his head. He couldn't do any of those things! Fluttershy was growing concerned. She should have just taken him home when she had the chance! Now her sweet Angel was being publicly humiliated. It was terrible.

Fluttershy raised her voice above her usual whisper. "Angel, let's go on home to the cottage now and—"

"Well, you must be able to do *something* special, little fellow!" Flam shouted, ignoring the yellow pony. This little display was entertaining the guests!

"Oh, he can do *lots* of things,"

Fluttershy defended him. She held her chin up and furrowed her brow. "He ... he ... gives the best cuddles! And he's great at keeping me on schedule." Fluttershy nodded her head. "I'm never late for anything when Angel is around." Angel took out his pocket watch and nodded his head.

Flim and Flam looked at each other and smirked. "That's all well and good, miss, but we only allow the *rarest* of rabbits and the *funniest* of bunnies to join our Farnum and Failey Top Hat Bunny Cabaret." Flim pointed to a plain brown rabbit in a scarecrow costume. "Even Foo Foo over there does a great routine with field mice!"

Flam gestured to Angel. "This bunny here has got nothing to offer us!"

"Oh," said Fluttershy, hanging her

head. "That's OK. We understand." She looked down at Angel. The poor dear had tears in his eyes. It broke Fluttershy's heart. Not even a cherry on top of Angel's salad tonight was going to fix this one. Fluttershy was just going to have to find some other way to make her favorite pet see himself for the special guy he most certainly was. But how?

CHAPTER 4

Taking Flock

It had taken Fluttershy all morning to convince Angel to pry himself out of his bed and come to Sweet Apple Acres with her. Luckily, it wasn't the first time she'd dealt with his moods, so she knew a few tricks. Today it was the promise of some carrot sorbet with sunflower seeds and an ear massage that had finally persuaded him to leave the cottage.

But he was still grumpy.

As sweet as Angel Bunny was, he was prone to pouting when he didn't get his way. Everything had to be just right – his tail had to be fluffed the exact way on Tail-Fluffing Tuesdays, his meals had to be arranged just so, and he had to spend at least one hour of exclusive playtime with Fluttershy every day. It was OK with her, though. Whatever he needed, she would give him. It was a vow that she made to all her pets and creatures.

Before the pony and the bunny had left, Angel had insisted he didn't feel like hopping, so Fluttershy had offered him the comfortable option of sitting on her back. "I'll try not to trot too

fast!" assured Fluttershy, lifting him up.
He wasn't heavy.

Fluttershy hummed a pretty tune as
they cantered along. When she was
finished, she looked over her shoulder to
check on Angel. He still seemed so sad.

"Cheer up! Applejack's invited us to
watch her and Winona practice for the
upcoming herding competition at
Whinnyland," Fluttershy said, softly
trotting toward the direction of the farm.
"It's part of the Furry Friends Fair. Won't
that be a nice time?"

The little bunny let out a big sigh and
collapsed dramatically, hiding his face in
Fluttershy's left wing. He gave a
halfhearted squeak into her feathers. He
stayed this way for the rest of the trip.

"My poor bunny! I know you're upset
about those big meanies Flim and Flam

* ✱ **25** ✱ *✱*

not letting you into their show," cooed
Fluttershy. "But *I* think you're special
enough to star in your own show. We
could throw something together. Maybe
Rarity will help us make some costumes?"

Angel hopped off Fluttershy's back
and shook his head defiantly. *No way!* he
seemed to say.

Sweet Apple Acres was coming into
view on the horizon. It was looking
particularly pretty today. The shining
green orchard was filled with trees full of
juicy red apples stretched out in rows up
and down the hills. The farmhouse where
Applejack, her siblings, Apple Bloom and
Big Mac, and their grandmare, Granny
Smith, lived was perched proudly in front,
looking over the bountiful land. The
massive red barn that the whole Apple
family had built with their own hooves

was off to the side. Just past that were several open fields, one of which Applejack and her pet dog Winona were currently practicing in.

Angel sprang off toward the field, still annoyed. Fluttershy followed, trying to rack her brain for something else that would make her pet feel better. A great idea would surely come to her soon.

"Hi, Applejack!" uttered Fluttershy,  not much louder than a whisper. Herding practice was already in full swing. There were a dozen fluffy white sheep shuffling around the pasture. Applejack was running along the edges of the fence.

"Get 'round, Winona!" Applejack

hollered across the field. Winona barked a reply, tail wagging like an overactive pendulum. Then the brown-and-white pup shot off toward the corner of the green expanse. She wove in and out of the herd of sheep, as nimble as Rainbow Dash zipping through a mass of puffy white clouds in the sky.

 Fluttershy couldn't believe how quick the two of them were! From the look on Angel's face, neither could he. He was up on the fence, leaning forward, totally captivated by the country pony's smooth moves. "Yay," Fluttershy cheered so softly that not even Angel heard her. "Go, Applejack!"

"Way to me, girl!" Applejack shouted at her dog, galloping around the sheep.

Winona didn't miss a beat. She charged around the flock in wide circles and brought them in closer to one another. "Baaaa!" they bleated as they dodged the duo. "Baaa! Baaaaaaa!"

"Walk up!" Applejack ran to the opposite side from Winona. The dog ran into the middle of the flock, and the formation exploded like fireworks. "Atta girl, Winona! Now go by. . . ." Applejack motioned with her hoof. Winona switched directions and ran clockwise around the sheep. At the top of the circle, she made a small detour inward each time. "Watch 'em!"

Winona stopped running and sat down. She didn't take her eyes off the flock. Her pink tongue hung out of her mouth as she panted heavily from the physical activity. The sheep remained where they were, blank looks on their faces. "Now drive 'em home, girl!" At this command, Winona ran around one more time, molding the formation into a perfect heart shape in the center of the field.

"Yee-haw!" Applejack shouted, standing up and kicking out her forelegs in glee. "That was a near perfect run, if I do say so mah-self! Whooo-eee!" She trotted over to Winona and patted her on the head. The pup barked and licked Applejack on the cheek.

"Angel, wait for me!" Fluttershy called out after her runaway bunny. The little guy had hopped right into the pasture and onto one of the sheep's backs! He looked like he was inspecting the sheep and trying to talk to her.

But the ewe just ignored the small bunny. She leaned her neck down to take a bite of the grass in front of her.

"Be careful!" Fluttershy winced as Angel slid down the sheep's neck and onto the ground. He dusted himself off and hopped over to Applejack and Winona, bouncing around them in excitement. What had suddenly gotten into him? Whatever it was, Fluttershy was glad he was feeling better. Some fresh air and pony friends always cheered her up.

"Howdy, Fluttershy," Applejack said with a smile and a tip of her signature brown cowpony hat. "Hiya there, Angel. Didn't see you two watchin' there. I was so caught up in our routine! How do y'all reckon we did?"

Angel smiled and reached his paws up high. "Looks like you got two paws-up from Angel!" Fluttershy giggled. Her pink mane fell across one eye. "And I thought it was just *wonderful*."

Applejack grinned at the praise. "Those competitors at the Whinnyland Herding Competition won't know what hit 'em, huh, Winona?" Applejack trotted over to one of the sheep and gave it a pat on its woolly head. "The Bleating Heart is a formation we've been trying to get right for ages. Somethin' finally clicked today with the flock."

"Beaeeaaa aaa aaahh," said one of the sheep in response.

"What a group of little sweeties,"

Fluttershy cooed to the fluffballs. "You all are very talented and should give yourselves a pat on the back! Or an extra-large helping of grass." Fluttershy nuzzled one of the sheep. "I can't wait to cheer for you at the competition. I'll yell extra loud to show my support."

"I'll be lookin' forward to that." Applejack chuckled. Everypony knew that Fluttershy's cheers could barely be called cheers, they were so quiet. It annoyed Rainbow Dash, but the rest of the ponies thought it was kind of funny. Fluttershy did her best to show her support.

Angel Bunny bounded over to the group of sheep eating grass in the middle of the field. The little white rabbit jumped in circles around two sheep, copying Winona's movements as best as he could. When nopony noticed, he began to pull on Applejack's tail to try and get her attention.

"What's that, little feller?" Applejack knelt down. Angel stomped his foot on the ground impatiently, then took off hopping around the sheep in another circle. He pointed to himself and then to Winona. She wagged her tail. Angel frowned.

"You want to play with Winona?" Fluttershy asked, cocking her head to the side. Angel shook his head. *No.* The bunny grabbed Fluttershy's hoof and brought her over to the sheep. Then he pushed her flank, trying to make her trot forward. "You want *me* to pet the sheep?"

Angel sighed. He pulled out a tiny cowpony hat and lasso and began to act like Applejack. *I want to do what Winona does!*

"Oh!" Fluttershy gasped, eyes wide with shock. She looked up at Applejack.

"I think…Angel Bunny…wants to enter the Whinnyland Herding Competition?"

Angel Bunny nodded with a cheesy grin and put both paws up in the air. Two paws-up. Fluttershy imagined the stadium filled with all those professional herding ponies and their dogs. She gulped. A  bunny and a very shy Pegasus, who had never learned a herding routine in their entire lives, against all of them? It sounded daunting, but it also sounded like an idea only a very special, talented bunny would have.

"OK…if it will make you happy, my little fluffy ball of love," Fluttershy squeaked, "we'll do it."

CHAPTER 5

Sheepbunny in Training

"Um, oh...uh...walk up?" Fluttershy called out the herding command.

"Or should that be 'hop up' since you're a bunny?"

Across the field, Angel strained to hear his pony. He perked his right ear up and cocked his head to the side in confusion.

"Oh, I'm sorry, Angel!" Fluttershy could feel beads of sweat forming on her forehead. It was a sunny day, but the perspiration was definitely a product of her nerves. Herding was really hard to do! Applejack and Winona made it look so easy. "I'll get it right soon, I promise, little dear."

The competition was being held at the Furry Friends Fair next week, so it didn't leave much time for the bunny to learn the art of sheep herding. Applejack and Winona had generously offered to lend Fluttershy and Angel the neighbouring field, as well as to demonstrate some of the basic commands. Though Fluttershy was still hesitant about the plan, she had never seen Angel so excited about anything!

Each morning before Princess Celestia rose the sun, Angel was already up and hippity-hopping about, doing his stretches and drinking shakes made of blended kale and celery. It seemed that he had all but forgotten the unkind words of those silly Flim Flam brothers. Whenever Fluttershy and Angel would pass through Ponyville Park, right by the circus tent on the way to Applejack's house, the bunny would hop past with his nose in the air. Those show bunnies had nothing on his new and unique talent.

That's why Fluttershy *had* to buck up and put on a brave face. For Angel.

"Why don't y'all try the Apple Crate formation again?" suggested Applejack, taking a swig of cold apple juice and hanging against the side of the pasture fence. "That one's real easy, I promise, sugarcube." Applejack gave a reassuring smile. "Go on...."

"OK," Fluttershy panted. "What does that one look like again?" She looked to the flock of sheep. They were all over the pasture. It was going to be a challenge just to get them in the same corner, let alone into a shape.

"Just what it sounds like." Applejack pointed to a small rectangle of red picket fence in the back of the field. "You just gotta get all the sheep into the enclosure, like apples in a crate. Simple as pie."

"Did I hear somepony say *pie*?!" Pinkie Pie shrieked as she bounced towards them, her bouncy fuchsia mane and tail billowing out with each jump.

Rarity and Twilight Sparkle trotted along behind her.

Applejack raised an eyebrow. "I *did* say it, but—"

"Woo-hoo! I love pie!" Pinkie licked her chops. "What kind are we having today?"

"I'm afraid you're the only pie in sight, Pinkie," Applejack said. She waved her hoof at the field. "Winona and I are busy teachin' Fluttershy here how to herd sheep with Angel Bunny." In the distance, Angel hopped in a circle around one of the sheep's legs. The ewe was completely uninterested and didn't budge.

"Aww! Guess I'll just have to eat this instead." Pinkie pouted, then procured a slice of pineapple upside-down cake out of nowhere. She grabbed Applejack's juice and took a sip. "Thanks, bestie!"

"Fluttershy, darling." Rarity stuck out her tongue in disgust. "Why ever would you want to herd sheep? I know you love animals, but sheep are by far the smelliest of the lot." She put her dainty, polished hoof up to her white nose. "In fact, if I'm going to stand here, I think I need my botanical hat for scent diffusion." Rarity placed a large sunhat covered with fragrant fresh flowers on her purple mane. She took a deep breath of their floral scent. "Yes, that's better."

"It's not me who wants to learn – it's my poor little Angel Bunny." Fluttershy hung her head. "It was those nasty Flim Flam brothers and their bunny cabaret. Angel wanted to join the show, but they said he had no special talents."

"Oh, I saw that show!" Pinkie chirped. "It was really good. I *love* that macaroni bunny." Pinkie turned to Rarity and Twilight. "Have you tried his three-cheese dish? Delectable-umptious."

"I heard that bunny trained at Le Fleur Garland – the best culinary academy in the world!" remarked Rarity. She turned to Twilight and explained, "When he's not performing in the show, he's been cooking over at that new restaurant, Grassy Mare Tavern—"

"You ponies are not exactly helping," Applejack barked. "Close yer pieholes!"

"Pie again, huh?" Pinkie Pie gave a suspicious look and rubbed her chin. "I think you might be hiding something, Applejack—"

"A guest bunny chef? See what my adorable little sweetheart is up against?" Fluttershy whimpered. "It's why he wants to enter the Whinnyland Herding

Competition – to show them that he can do something."

"But Angel can do lots of things!" insisted Pinkie Pie. "Gummy says he tells the best jokes!" She pointed to her pet  baby alligator. "Tell them that one Angel made up about the spoon and the garden gnome!" The little guy showed no reaction except for blinking a few times. Pinkie giggled and turned to her friends. "Good one, huh?"

Everypony exchanged a confused look. Pinkie Pie continued to roll around on the grass with laughter.

"I tried to tell him that I already think he's the most wonderful bunny in the world, but he won't believe me!"

Fluttershy whimpered again. "Well, I guess I better get back to work." Fluttershy took off toward the bunny. From afar, the ponies could see her rubbing his ear and trying to make him drink a juice box. He refused and kept hopping around, gesturing to the sheep.

Twilight Sparkle wore a look of concern as she watched the pitiful scene. "Is a bunny even allowed to enter the competition? I thought it was just for Earth ponies and their dogs."

"Traditionally, yes." Applejack nodded. "But I looked up the rules, and it's not that specific. Just says no flyin', and ya have to use the herdin' phrases. So long as Fluttershy doesn't use her wings and Angel follows the traditional canine commands, he can compete."

The ponies watched as Fluttershy and Angel did a hopeless dance of hopping around the flock, barely getting one sheep out of the whole bunch to move.

Finally, two sheep walked forward. "Beeaa aaah!" they bleated.

"Oh, look!" Rarity exclaimed. "Those two moved! Maybe there *is* hope for Fluttershy and Angel's routine." The ewes bent down and began to rip large mouthfuls of grass out of the earth. As they chewed, they sank to the ground and lay down for a rest. One of them fell asleep. "Oh. Never mind."

"In all my herdin' days, I ain't ever seen a flock disobey the routine like that!" Applejack marvelled. "Not even Braeburn's dog, Albus. And that pup's come in last place at every competition."

"It's like Fluttershy's voice is actually putting them to sleep!" Pinkie Pie's eyes widened. All but one of the sheep had curled up on the grass for a nap. "Oooooo. That's actually pretty cool...."

"My little lambies, my little lambies..." Fluttershy began to sing. *"Listen to Angeeeel."*

"I don't know, girls." Twilight bit her lip. "Fluttershy might be in over her head with this one."

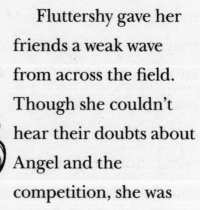

Fluttershy gave her friends a weak wave from across the field. Though she couldn't hear their doubts about Angel and the competition, she was having just as many herself. She wanted to make Angel happy – but at some point, she needed to put her hoof down and tell him that it just wasn't working. A bunny could do a lot of amazing things, but being a sheepdog was not one of them.

CHAPTER 6

The Warm, Fuzzy Truth

Fluttershy was terrible at telling ponies the truth, especially if there was the slightest chance that she might hurt their feelings. Unfortunately, this fact also applied to bunnies. Three whole days had passed since she'd decided to talk to Angel about dropping out of the herding competition at Whinnyland and she still hadn't brought it up! Fluttershy had continued taking him to herding practise in between her duties caring for all the other animals at the cottage. The longer she waited, the worse it felt.

"Angel, dear," said Fluttershy, following her quick bunny through the center of Ponyville. "How about we go for a nice lunch at the café instead of going to the farm? I'm sure you must be getting very tired from all that hopping around…"

The bunny didn't even stop. He surged forward, eager to give his herding routine another try. He turned his head over his fuzzy white shoulder. *Come on, Fluttershy!*

"Oh, all right." Fluttershy nodded and followed him. Maybe after today's practise she would *gently* suggest that they pull out of the competition. Then the two of them could get back to their normal lives. Out of the spotlight and safe from public humiliation.

"What's up, Fluttershy?! I haven't seen you in ages!" Rainbow Dash darted over and landed beside her. "Is everything OK? You seem jumpy." Rainbow gave her the side-eye. "I mean, more so than usual. You're always kinda jumpy."

"I'm OK…" Fluttershy's eyes darted around to make sure Angel was out of earshot. "It's just that I've been busy trying to help Angel Bunny train for the Furry Friends Fair sheep herding competition."

"The one at Whinnyland?" Rainbow

replied. "Man, I love it there! All the awesome games and thrilling rides! I can't wait to ride the new roller coaster, the Radical Rainboom. Lightning Dust said it's even better than the Dizzitron."

"That *does* sound exciting," Fluttershy agreed. "I wish *I* was going to the fair just to have fun…" She looked to the ground and gave a huge sigh.

Rainbow Dash crossed her forelegs over her chest. "Let me guess – you don't want to be in the herding competition?"

"If I'm being honest…" Fluttershy craned her neck and looked around again. She lowered her voice to the tiniest whisper possible. *"No."*

"Yeah, I thought so. I heard you were having trouble," Rainbow Dash admitted. "Maybe you should switch it up. Try some cows instead?"

"The sheep aren't so bad," Fluttershy lied. "They're little sweethearts. I just wish they would listen to me and Angel just a little *teensy-weensy, tiny* bit better." A look of guilt flashed across her face. "But don't tell them that. I know they're trying their best."

"But it's still not working, right?" Rainbow Dash replied. She scratched her rainbow mane. "What can we do to get a flock of sheep to listen to you and Angel?"

"I don't know if we can!" cried Fluttershy. "Maybe I should finally tell Angel that we're dropping out."

"Don't throw in the towel just yet!" Rainbow Dash smirked. She put her hooves on her hips triumphantly. "If anypony can whip you two into shape, it's *me*."

☆ ☆ ☆

"OK, gang! Listen up!" Rainbow Dash shouted. "Birds – you guys, too!"

An eruption of twitters and tweets came from the branches of the nearby apple trees. Rainbow grinned. "I hope it's OK that I invited the birds."

"Oh, of course." Fluttershy smiled. She actually felt a little better with her feathered friends around. "Hello, my sweet little winged friends. I hope you're feeling welcomed and loved."

"All right! So anyway…" Rainbow Dash paced back and forth in front of her five best friends like Spitfire did with the recruits at the Wonderbolt Academy. After coaching the Ponyville teams for the Equestria Games, Rainbow Dash had got really good at giving inspirational pep talks. Especially ones involving a sport.

"Fluttershy and Angel need us to watch their herding practice and tell them what exactly they're doing wrong." Rainbow puffed out her chest. "Then they'll be able to fix it and become the most awesome herding team there is!"

Angel jumped up and down in glee. The birds chirped and sang. Winona barked. And Applejack furrowed her brow. "Except…"

"Except Applejack and Winona, of course," Twilight said with a wink.

"Aw, I'm just messin' around." Applejack laughed. "Let's get started!"

An hour and several herding trials later, the ponies all

understood why Fluttershy was such a
wreck. As much as Angel wanted to be a
sheepbunny, the little guy was terrible at
listening to the commands Fluttershy was
calling out. He had always been naughty
and liked to do things on his own terms.
The trouble was – herding was most
definitely a team sport! Angel was too
small to see which direction to hop in on
his own. He needed Fluttershy to help
him gather the sheep into the right
formations. The two of them already had
a near psychic connection, so why
couldn't they get this right?

Rainbow Dash blew her whistle. "Why
doesn't everysheep take five?"

"BaaaaaaAHH," the sheep bleated in
response, then continued not paying the
ponies any attention at all.

Fluttershy trotted over, sweat trickling

down her sweet yellow face. "Was that any better?" She batted her dark eyelashes.

"You want the honest truth?" Applejack asked with a trace of hesitation. She was going to give it anyway.

"Go on, I can take it," Fluttershy whimpered. She looked back over her shoulder at Angel.

"It stunk worse than a pigpen on a hot—"

Rarity stuck her hoof over Applejack's mouth. "I think what A.J. *means* is, it wasn't quite up to par yet, darling. But you'll get there!"

"Oooh, I have an idea!" said Pinkie Pie, springing up from the grass. "Maybe the sheepies need to be sheared. I bet they can't hear Fluttershy and Angel through all that fluffy-wuffy wool."

"It's true. Wool *does* absorb sound quite well." Rarity nodded. "That's why it's the perfect fabric for librarians to wear. Which actually reminds me of this one outfit I dreamed up for Twilight—"

"Come on, Pinkie," Rainbow Dash interrupted with a smirk. "It's *Fluttershy* giving the commands. I think we all know why they can't hear her!"

The ponies all giggled. Fluttershy *was* very soft-spoken.

"Oh, it's no use!" Fluttershy cried, sinking to the ground. She let out a sniffle. "I can't do this. I...I...give up!" In the distance, Angel's long ears drooped down to the ground. He could hear her just fine after all.

CHAPTER 7

Sugarcube Cornered

Sugarcube Corner was bustling with ponies. Sugar Rush Hour always took place right after the Ponyville Schoolhouse was released for the day, and sure enough, the fillies and colts were lined up straight out the door for their afternoon sweet treats. Applejack, Rarity, Twilight Sparkle and Rainbow Dash all had their spoons at the ready when Pinkie Pie set the gigantic banana split down on the table in front of Fluttershy.

"There ya go, Fluttershy," Pinkie Pie singsonged. "A triple-whipped, six-flavour, quadruple-whammy-jammy Lickety Split with extra nuts and sprinkles! Oh, and a chimi-cherry on top! Hope this will be yummy in your tummy after that tough practice today." Pinkie whipped out a huge neon-pink spoon. "Mind if I have a taste?"

"Go right ahead, Pinkie Pie." Fluttershy pushed the frozen dessert over. "I don't feel that hungry anyway." She lowered her sad eyes to the table. "But thank you for the kind gesture."

"Cheer up, Fluttershy! I'm sure Angel Bunny will understand if you two don't compete," Twilight offered. She gave her friend a reassuring pat on the back. "You two can just enjoy the Furry Friends Fair instead. Has he ever ridden the Bunny-Go-Round at Whinnyland?"

"No, but…" Fluttershy sniffed. "How will Angel Bunny know that he's the most special, most wonderful, bestest bunny a pony can have if he doesn't get to achieve his dreams? And *I'm* the pony who squashed them!"

"Oh, it's not as bad as all that, sugarcube," said Applejack, taking a bite of chocolate ice cream and banana. "It's just a silly ol' contest!"

"Then why are *you* competing in it, huh?" Rainbow Dash leaned in close to Applejack's face. Those two loved to challenge each other over every little thing.

Applejack scoffed. "Because –

unlike Fluttershy and Angel here – me 'n' Winona are true farmers. *We've* been herding stock since the cows came home!"

"You're right, Applejack," Fluttershy said, shaking her head, causing her pink mane to gently sway. "I'm not a farmer pony at all. And this is the first time I haven't been able to get a group of animals to listen to me." She looked at her friends. "I wish … I wish … that one of *you* could compete with Angel."

Everypony turned to Applejack with their eyebrows raised in hope.

"No can do, honeycrisp." Applejack shrugged. "I'm already signed up to compete with Winona. Only one trial per pony, I'm afraid. Rarity?"

"Moi?" Rarity gave a nervous laugh. "Compete in a field with livestock?" She took a dainty nibble of vanilla ice cream. "What about somepony more sporty, like Rainbow Dash? Surely she would do a much better job than me."

They all looked to Rainbow Dash. "Are you kidding me?! It's an Earth pony sport! I'd get disqualified right out of the gate for accidentally going superfast with my wings." Rainbow shrugged. "Can't help it. I think Pinkie Pie here is the obvious choice."

"I'd love to!" shrieked Pinkie Pie, springing out of her chair like she'd been launched by a catapult. Everypony smiled. When she landed, Pinkie Pie turned to

Fluttershy. "But I can't."

"What?" said all the ponies in unison.

"Why not?" Rainbow Dash crossed her forelegs across her chest like she was personally offended that her great idea didn't pan out.

"I'm already competing with Fluttershy's chickens in the Furry Friends Fair chicken dance contest." Pinkie giggled. "I already had my chicken suit dry-cleaned and everything."

Pinkie whipped out her chicken costume, which was on a wire hanger with plastic sheeting over it. "See?"

"Really? Elizabeak didn't even tell me!" Fluttershy lamented. "I have been so busy with the practices. My poor little chickens…"

"Don't worry," Pinkie Pie assured her. "They're doing great. Except sometimes

Henrita can be such a drama queen, you know? Anyway, if I can't do it, that only leaves one pony!" Pinkie pointed her hoof at the purple princess who had her mouth full of banana-and-strawberry ice cream. "Twilight."

The ponies all turned their attention to Twilight Sparkle, who looked around in confusion. "What? Me? *I* can't compete with Angel," Twilight explained. "I'm sorry, Fluttershy, but royals aren't allowed. It wouldn't be fair to the other contestants."

"Oh, that does make sense..." replied Fluttershy, slumping down. "It's OK. I understand. I'll see you all later." She stood up and trotted over to the door, her yellow hooves gently clip-clopping against the pale green tiles. "After I break the bad news to Angel Bunny."

Rarity, Rainbow Dash, Pinkie Pie, Applejack and Twilight all felt awful as they watched their sweet, kind friend walk out the door.

"Poor Fluttershy." Rarity sighed. "If only there were something else we could do to help out so that she'll be more comfortable in the sheep herding competition!"

"Maybe there is," Twilight replied, brightening. "And I think it starts with a trip to the Crystal Empire."

The ponies all started talking at once.

"FUN!" Pinkie Pie squealed, jumping up and down. Suddenly, she stopped herself. "Wait. Why are we going to the Crystal Empire?"

"If you're all in . . ." Twilight said, "I'm going to need some help wrangling a herd of tiny ewes."

Twilight smiled at her friends. This plan was going to be perfect.

CHAPTER 8

Ewe Can Do It, Fluttershy!

"Traaaalalalala tweet, it's time to eat!
Traalalala loo, you're invited, too!" As
Fluttershy sang, flittering around her
cottage, she began to feel a teensy bit
better. She filled up ceramic dishes with
cool water, restocked the bird feeders
with fresh seeds, and fluffed the pillows

of all forty-two of the current animals' beds.

"There you go, my little loves," Fluttershy cooed to some hamsters that were scurrying over to a bowl of fresh food. A bluebird landed on her shoulder and nuzzled her face. *Tweet, tweet, tweet!* "It's good to see you, too, Judy," Fluttershy replied, smoothing down her pretty feathers. "I've missed you all so much!"

The bird took off out the open window as another flew in. "Hello, Hummingway!" Fluttershy chirped. Her cottage was full of happy animals. Currently, there was just one creature who wasn't pleased with Fluttershy. Poor little Angel had been upset about the news, but said he understood.

"Do you need anything in there, Angel?" Fluttershy whispered, peeking through the opening of his bunny tepee – a few sticks propped up surrounded by a blankie in the middle of the living room. "Some more pillows? A magazine?"

Angel pursed his lips together and shook his head. "Well, just ring the bell if you do, sweetie." It broke her heart to see him sulking, but Fluttershy knew that pulling out of the contest was the right thing to do. If the two of them had gone out onto the field at the fair, they would have become a laughing stock! A *livestock* laughing stock. And that would have been much worse for Angel's confidence. Really, Fluttershy was just protecting him and his delicate little soul.

A knock came at the door. Fluttershy

gently placed a grey kitten on the floor near a dish of milk and flew over. "Just hold tight, Sneezy. I'll be right back." The kitten sneezed in response.

When she opened the door, Fluttershy saw all five of her friends and a flock of eight tiny Crystal Empire ewes! "What's all this about?" Fluttershy marvelled. The sparkling glint of their crystal wool looked brilliant in the sunshine.

"We brought you ewes to use!" Pinkie Pie cheered with a smile. She turned to Rainbow Dash. "Or was it, use these ewes so you don't lose?" She held a pink leash with a tiny blush-colored ewe at the end of it. The little fluffy creature looked like a cloud of cotton candy. "Either way," said Pinkie Pie, "aren't they adorable?"

"Baaaaah," the tiny pink sheep bleated with a smile.

"Look, I gave mine a cape," Rarity said. Her purple ewe held her muzzle up with an air of sophistication and posed, showing off a rhinestone silver garment. Rarity giggled. "Fabulous, no?"

"My goodness!" Fluttershy exclaimed, trotting forward to pet the little dears. They were so soft and pretty, with pastel purple, blue, and pink wool. "I haven't seen these lovely lambies since the Equestria Games," Fluttershy added, brightening. A few of the Crystal ewes walked over and started nuzzling Fluttershy's legs. She giggled in delight. "Hello there. I remember you!"

"Even though none of us can take your place with Angel in the herding competition, we thought maybe you two could use some help. We checked the rules and it doesn't say anything about the size of the sheep!" said Twilight Sparkle. She passed Fluttershy a purple leash and the matching lavender ewe. "Giving up would be silly after you two have worked so hard."

"And we've put together a few other treats to help y'all out, too." Applejack grinned. "Come on back with us to Sweet Apple Acres and see 'em!"

"Wow, this is all really nice of you ponies, but…" Fluttershy stopped for a moment and looked at the ground. "But…" The ponies all leaned in with anticipation. Was she going to give it another shot or not? "But…"

"Out with it already!" Rainbow Dash shouted.

"But I'm going to have to check with Angel first," admitted Fluttershy.

"Something tells me he's going to be on board...." Twilight laughed. She pointed to Angel Bunny, who was smiling and chasing a blue Crystal ewe down the path. Fluttershy breathed a sigh of relief. Everything was going to be much better now that Angel had some sheep his own size. Plus, now they had their own personal cheering squad in the form of the five best pony friends a girl could have.

CHAPTER 9

The Furry Friends Fair

The ponies took the train past
Manehattan to arrive at the Whinnyland
Boardtrot in the morning, leaving
enough time to catch a few rides, play
some games, and dip their tired hooves in
the sparkling sea before it was time to get
ready for the big competition. Fluttershy,

however, was far too nervous to play or eat caramel popcorn.

She and Angel decided it would be much better to rest in the competitors' tent, taking care of the tiny Crystal ewes until the afternoon. That way, they would be ready to face the crowd with their brand-new routine when it was their turn.

Fluttershy was trying not to let her nerves rub off on Angel, but it was so hard! She had always had a difficult time in front of crowds, whether it was just to help Ponyville's Pegasi lift the water to Cloudsdale by creating a tornado or singing with the Pony Tones quartet. She'd done well competing in the relay at the Equestria Games, but it was as if she'd spent all her confidence on that one event.

"Are you sure you don't want to come and ride the Radical Rainboom with me and Lightning Dust?" Rainbow Dash asked one last time. The sounds of ponies screaming on the rides could be heard outside. "It might just be the best thing that's *ever* going to happen!" The rainbow Pegasus was practically vibrating with excitement. "Like, ever."

"No, thank you, Rainbow Dash," Fluttershy said, shifting from hoof to hoof and finally taking a seat next to a purple ewe. She began to pet her. "But I hope you have a nice time."

Rainbow looked at her sideways. "I hope you're not staying here to do some more practising, 'cause ever since I got

Spitfire to come to Ponyville to coach you and Angel, you guys have got it *down*."

Rainbow Dash took off like a rocket toward the boardtrot to get in line for the Radical Rainboom.

A few moments later, Twilight Sparkle and Rarity stopped in. Twilight smiled at Fluttershy. "We were just going to get some apple fritter funnel cakes. Do you want to come?"

"No, no really," Fluttershy insisted, peeking her eyes outside the tent. Hundreds of ponies and their furry friends were starting to fill the benches. Fluttershy could feel her heart beating a little faster. "I just want to stay here for now and rest."

"If you insist, darling," Rarity tutted, and raised a suspicious eyebrow. "Just don't forget to put on your costumes before it's your turn to go out on the field, OK? They are really going to add a little something to the performance – *trust me*."

"We won't forget, will we, Angel?" Fluttershy patted him on the head. The bunny held up his brand-new sky-blue velveteen vest and nodded his head vigorously. *I won't forget!* It was cute to see how excited Angel was about his big day.

"Oh, I knew he would love velvet," Rarity gushed. "Just the right fabric to make a rabbit look dapper."

"Yes, it's very nice. Now go ahead, and I'll see you girls later," Fluttershy said, pushing her friends out of the tent. What did a pony have to do to get some peace and quiet around here? "I'm just going to get ready."

"OK," said Twilight, looking back over her shoulder. She whispered something to Rarity as the two ponies left.

"Phew," said Fluttershy, looking at Angel.

"Those ponies sure do fuss a lot. What should we do now that they're gone?"

Angel pointed to his watch and then to the costume rack, where Fluttershy's dress was hanging. It was a frilly get-up, complete with a blue bonnet, a lace dress with puffy white sleeves, and a staff decorated with  blue bows. Fluttershy winced. It was a little bit *much* for her simple taste, but she had to wear it. She didn't want to hurt Rarity's feelings.

All her friends had been so nice in arranging special treats to help her overcome her fear of the competition. Twilight had brought her the tiny ewes, Rainbow Dash had rallied Spitfire to coach them, Rarity had sewn the costumes, Pinkie Pie had been their constant cheerleader, and Applejack had built a special tiny sheep pen for the new flock. They were all so generous. What if she failed them? Her heart started to beat fast, and she began to hyperventilate.

Angel cocked his head to the side. He looked worried and a little more nervous himself. Fluttershy took a deep breath and composed herself.

"Phew. OK, you're right, Angel," Fluttershy said. "I should probably get dressed." She grabbed the outfit and nuzzled Angel's nose. "Watch the ewes while I go put this on, OK, little sweetie? I'll be right back."

But ten minutes later,

when Fluttershy returned to the tent covered head to hoof in frilly lace, the flock of Crystal ewes was gone! And so was Angel Bunny.

CHAPTER 10

Alone at the Fair

The Furry Friends Fair was in full swing.
Fluttershy couldn't believe how many
entertaining things were available for
ponies and their pets. There was a kitty
show, pet food stands, and games the
ponies could play to win prizes and treats
for their animal buddies. It was difficult for

Fluttershy not to get distracted looking at all the adorable creatures. But she was on a mission to find her bunny and her sheep.

"Angel?" Fluttershy trotted down the aisles of the fairground, making her way through the heaving crowd of ponies. "Where did you hop off to?"

She pushed her way past a game booth for doggies. It launched colourful balls out to the players, who in turn tried to catch them in their mouths. The dog who caught the most won a prize. Fluttershy noticed one of the dogs from her picture in the herding trials program – her name was Scout, and the stout brown stallion next to her must be her owner, Corral. His cutie mark was a whistle, and he wore a black cowpony hat.

Scout was declared the winner and barked happily as she chose her prize

– a squeaky, stuffed cow chew toy with a bell around its neck. "Good girl, Scout!" said Corral, patting her on the head. "Now it's time to go compete. You ready to herd some sheep?" Scout did a backflip, and the two ran off towards the fields. *Wow,* thought Fluttershy.

The yellow pony bit her lip. Time was running out. Somepony around here had to have seen her pets! Fluttershy tapped the shoulder of a pink Unicorn mare. "Um, excuse me, miss?" she said softly.

The Unicorn turned around and gave her a funny look. "Are you talking to me?"

"Um, yes, if that's OK." Fluttershy bowed her head. "See, I've lost my sheep, and I was wondering if you might have seen them anywhere. See, we're going to be late for—"

"Oh, *I* get it!" The Unicorn started laughing. She tapped her friend – a white Earth pony with a green mane – on the shoulder. "Look, it's one of those plays with the actors who talk to you! It's Little Pony Peep!"

The pony with the green mane looked at Fluttershy's costume and giggled. "And you've lost your sheep?"

"Well, yes, actually," Fluttershy replied, eyes darting around. "But I'm not an actor. I really did lose them. And my bunny, Angel…"

"Riiiiight." The pink Unicorn winked, playing along. "Though if you're going for authenticity, I don't think Little Pony Peep had a bunny in the story."

"Oh, um," Fluttershy replied, backing away. "Thank you. Bye."

Fluttershy looked around the busy fairground and suddenly felt hopeless. She was never going to find Angel in time! Everypony was going to be so disappointed. She began to trudge back towards the fields when she heard some very silly music. It sounded familiar...

"Why do I know this song?" said Fluttershy, trotting over to the bandstand. There was a stage set up, and tons of ponies were watching and stomping their hooves to the beat. Fluttershy pushed her way to the front. Up onstage was none other than Pinkie Pie dressed as a chicken! She had five of Fluttershy's chickens clucking around next to her, dancing with their wings. Elizabeak was even wearing a sparkling boa!

In the front row was Angel Bunny, sitting between eight tiny Crystal ewes. They were all bouncing back and forth in time with the music. They didn't look nervous at all! Suddenly, she realized that what she'd been thinking about the competition this entire time was wrong.

"Maybe I'm the one who's been making everysheep stressed out," Fluttershy said aloud to herself. "The Furry Friends Fair is supposed to be fun. It's no big deal what everypony else  thinks, as long as Angel and I have a good time together."

"That's what we've been trying to tell you all along, sugarcube!" said Applejack, bouncing next to her.

Twilight, Rarity, and Rainbow Dash all joined her, nodding their heads.

"Now, are you ready to have a good time?!" Applejack hollered.

"Absolutely!" replied Fluttershy with a smile. "I, um, just have to go round up my sheep first." She pointed her staff at the

tiny flock. They were all bleating happily for Pinkie Pie and the chickens, who were taking their final bows.

"Oh, darling." Rarity gasped. "Hearing you say those words while wearing that costume has shown me how misguided the whole look was! I must have been accidentally thinking about one of Sweetie Belle's old nursery rhymes.

Please don't wear it!"

"Phew." Fluttershy sighed. "I'm really glad you said that."

Angel Bunny hopped up to Fluttershy and nuzzled her leg. Then he pulled out his pocket watch and looked at it, and his eyes grew huge. Angel pulled down on his ears in shock.

We're going to be late!

"Not if I have anything to say about it." Fluttershy puffed up. "Angel...go by!"

The little bunny saluted Fluttershy and hopped off toward his tiny flock. He drove them all to the field without a single hitch.

CHAPTER 11

Trials and Errors

"That was Cromwell with his border collie, Ripley!" the announcer pony bellowed into the microphone. "All the way from Vanhoover!" The ponies in the stands whistled and hooted, waving little flags showing their support for the farm ponies and their pups. Cromwell, a grey

Earth pony stallion wearing a newsboy cap and a plaid vest, looked satisfied as he trotted off the field with his happy brown dog. Their routine had been simple, but perfectly executed. Both Applejack and Fluttershy were starting to feel the pressure.

"Do y'all think he did better than Cousin Braeburn and little Albus? Or Spring Song with that fluffy white pooch, Pearl?" Applejack asked, looking at her programme. There were only a few minutes left before her turn. Last up would be Fluttershy and Angel.

"Spring Song and Pearl had great style, but I think the team to beat is that pony Corral and his dog, Scout," Rarity enthused. "Did you see those backflips she did in a circle to round up the flock? *Très magnifique!*"

"It's called the Flip Pup Loop." Twilight nodded in agreement. She held up a dusty old book with a sheep on the cover. "And according to this book on the history of sheepdog trials in Trotland and Bales, it's a manoeuvre that's hardly ever attempted in competition based on its difficulty factor of eleven-point-five."

"Well, the Bleating Heart is a twelve!" said Applejack proudly. Winona wagged her tail. "We got this, girl."

"Everypony, please welcome Applejack and her dog, Winonaaaaaa!"

"Woo-hooo!" cheered Pinkie Pie, still wearing her chicken costume. "I mean, *cluck, cluck!*"

"You can do it, darlings!" shouted Rarity, waving a sparkling flag with an apple on it.

"Complete all your elements

correctly!" Twilight giggled, holding up the book. "It says the elements are the most important part!"

Over the next fifteen minutes, Winona darted and dashed. Applejack called and corralled. The dog and pony swerved through the sheep to create amazing lines and shapes. Applejack read the flock perfectly, calling out commands and staying quiet when she needed to.

When there was just one minute left on the clock, the whole audience held their breath as Winona wound around the flock, molding the fluffy sheep into a perfect heart shape. Then Winona barked three times, and the whole flock let out one big *"Baaaaaah!"* together.

"I don't believe it!" the announcer shouted into the microphone. "The Bleating Heart! Nopony in the history of the Whinnyland Herding Association has ever performed this element!" He laughed in wonder. "Now I've really seen it all, fillies and gentlecolts." Little did he know, he was about to see something else equally unbelievable – in the form of a shy yellow Pegasus and a tiny white bunny who were taking the centre of the field.

Fluttershy trotted down the line of tiny ewes and gave little words of encouragement to each one. "You're going to be great! Have fun! I love you!" When she got to the front of the flock, she turned to the whole group. "Um, I just want to say that no matter what happens out there, I'm proud of all of you."

She brushed her pink mane away from

her face and looked to Angel, who was jumping up and down with anticipation. He was ready to go. "Especially you, my sweet little guy. I'm lucky to have such a talented bunny as you as a friend." She nuzzled his face.

Their moment was interrupted by the music signalling the next contestant. The announcer's voice echoed through the speakers. "And last but not least, Fluttershy and Angel Bunny from Ponyville!"

Fluttershy looked to her friends one last time. They gave her reassuring nods, and Rainbow Dash pushed her out onto the

field. "Don't forget to smiiiiiiiiiiiiile!" shrieked Pinkie Pie.

The meek yellow Pegasus bit her lip as she trotted out, wondering what the crowd's reaction might be when the crowd realized Angel wasn't a sheepdog. The small bunny hopped out after her with his pink nose held high. He adjusted his blue vest and turned to the audience. Angel gave a deep bow with a flourish and took his place across the field from the pretty herd of tiny Crystal ewes.

A wave of whispers and a rustling of papers rolled through the crowd. The ponies checked their programmes in confusion. "Wow! Would you ponies look at that?" the announcer marvelled. "It appears we have a Furry Friends Fair first – a bunny is going to herd sheep! Miniature Crystal ewes at that!"

The audience erupted in laughter.

Fluttershy started to shake. She felt like flying straight off the field and back into the tent. But a second later, the whistle blew, and Angel looked to her for a command. It was showtime! *I can do this,* she told herself. *For Angel.*

"W-w-w-way to me, Bunny," whispered Fluttershy, pointing her hoof at the flock. More laughter came from the stands.

Angel nodded and darted off toward the sheep. Fluttershy had never seen him look so happy in his life. From that point on, it was easy. Fluttershy trotted and smiled, calling out to Angel. "Steady!" she commanded. "Hop up!"

The tiny Crystal ewes sparkled in the sunlight as they ran around the field, following the lead of their unlikely herding team. And the audience grew more and more quiet as they watched the bunny leap and hop his way to a beautiful finish, penning the eight tiny ewes in the custom gates in a perfect two-by-two arrangement.

The buzzer sounded, signalling their time was up.

"Folks – have you ever seen anything so astonishing?" the announcer bellowed in his deep voice. "Give a round of applause for Fluttershy and Angel – the amazing sheepherding bunny rabbit!"

Everypony's jaw was still practically on the ground from shock. It was almost a full minute of silence before the ponies began cheering and stomping their hooves on the ground in appreciation of the little bunny and his pony. "And that concludes the twenty-eighth annual Whinnyland Herding Competition! What a finish!"

Fluttershy grinned. This rush was better than riding the Radical Rainboom!

"We did it!" Fluttershy hugged Angel Bunny and swung him around. "See? You're the most special, talented bunny ever! Not because you did the routine perfectly but because you followed what was in your heart and didn't let anypony stop you from achieving your goal." Fluttershy knelt down to him. "I think that's what makes you the best bunny of all."

Angel smiled wide. *Thank you, Fluttershy.*

CHAPTER 12

Singing a Different Tune

A few days later, Mayor Mare held a big celebration in the Ponyville town square for the winners of the herding competition. DJ Pon-3 was playing music, and everypony was dancing and drinking apple juice. Two of their own had beaten the best sheepherders in Equestria!

Even though first place had gone to Winona and Applejack, it seemed Angel was so happy that he had not taken off his red second-place ribbon since the competition. Mayor Mare presented the winners to the town, and Fluttershy stood up on the stage next to Angel. She wasn't even the slightest bit nervous.

When the Pony Tones quartet got up onstage to sing a celebratory tune, Fluttershy even joined in for a few verses! *"When you do, doobie-do, what's in your heart-heart-apple cart!"* they sang. *"The sky's no limit, for what you can do, do, doobie-do!"* The Pony Tones swayed back and forth. Angel Bunny danced around with his red ribbon. *"Whether you're flat-hoofed, feathered, or furred . . . You, you, just youuuuu . . . You've got the stuff, shoobie-do-wop, to lead the herd!"*

When the song ended, two tall ponies with red manes made their way to the front. One of them had a mustache. The residents of Ponyville knew that neither of them was to be trusted. "Say, Mayor Mare, is that a special bunny you've got up there?"

The mayor looked down at Flim and Flam through her glasses. "Well, yes. Angel Bunny's just won—"

"He looks marvelous!" said Flim.

"Fabulous!" chirped Flam.

"Glorious!" they said together.

"Young pony, I've got a proposition for you! Would you like your pet to join our incredible bunny cabaret?" Flam leaned in close to Fluttershy. "We're always on the search for new talent!"

Flim winked. "Rising stars like him!"

"Oh, I don't know. Well, um... Angel?" Fluttershy turned to Angel.

He looked up at her with wide, intense eyes. Then the little bunny turned straight to the two brothers, stuck his tongue out, and shook his head.

Everypony laughed.

"Come on, pal!" Flim begged. "We'll put on a whole new show just for you."

"Ahem." Fluttershy cleared her throat and turned to Flim and Flam with a sly smile. "*No*," she said, loud enough for everypony in the whole town to hear.

"Woo-hoo! Go, Fluttershy!"

"Tell 'em!"

As the ponies pushed Flim and Flam away from the crowd, Angel jumped up next to the DJ booth and started to spin a tune. DJ Pon-3 smiled and stepped aside, letting the bunny try his paw at a new skill.

"This song is awesome!" Rainbow Dash exclaimed, shaking her tail back and forth to the beat. "Angel's a pretty sweet spinner."

"Looks like you might have a sheepherding, *DJ* bunny on your hooves now!" Twilight Sparkle laughed, bobbing her head in time with the music. Applejack, Rarity, and Pinkie Pie joined in, and soon everypony in the whole town was dancing.

"Maybe…" Fluttershy giggled. "I bet there's all sorts of new skills he'll want to try out now. I don't care if he herds sheep or bakes cookies or makes music. As long as he's doing what he loves, he'll always be number one to me."

"That'll do, Fluttershy," said Applejack with a smirk. "That'll do."

Read on for a sneak peek
of the next exciting
My Little Pony adventure,

Princess Celestia and the Royal Rescue

The sunlight dappled across the castle
floor in multicoloured shards, softening
the appearance of the checkered stones
with warmth and energy.

The gentle haze of daybreak had
always been Princess Celestia's favourite
time. Not just because she was in charge
of raising the sun. To her, the dawn was a
peaceful and quiet promise of things to
come – activities of the exciting day still
lay ahead of all the ponies in the land.
Today would be a beautiful sunrise.

Celestia turned to the sun and focussed her magic. She watched the progression of the golden orb climbing higher into the sky, turning her attention back to the pattern projected onto the floor every so often with the care of an artist creating a grand masterpiece. Even though this picture was one that the princess had painted the same way each morning for hundreds of moons, she gave it the same care every single day. It was her honour and duty.

The pieces of stained glass set in the centre of the main arched window depicted Equestria's newest princess – an exceptionally talented young scholar named Princess Twilight Sparkle. The new royal and her five best pony friends and dragon assistant, whose images were immortalized in the glass as well, had protected Equestria from peril on more than one occasion. They now nobly sought to spread the true spirit of the Elements of Harmony and, in turn, the Magic of Friendship across its lands. Twilight Sparkle, Rainbow Dash, Rarity, Pinkie Pie, Applejack, Fluttershy, and Spike had come a long way since they'd all become friends. Celestia beamed with pride whenever the young heroes graced her thoughts or when their image caught her attention.

A prominent piece of purple glass in the window cast a glow in the shape of a star on the centre tile of the floor, signalling that the morning sunrise was almost complete. Celestia closed her almond-shaped eyes, and her dark lashes pressed down against her white cheekbones. She mustered every inch of strength in her body. She felt herself glistening with magical energy, from the bottom of her gilded hooves to the edges of her flowing mane of lavender, pale green and periwinkle blue and bursting out to the very tip of her long, pearled horn. When Celestia opened her eyes again, the sun had reached the highest peak of its arc in the sky. The world was bright.

"*Gratias ad solis ortum*," the princess recited as she bowed deeply to the sun. "Thank you for allowing me to guide you, and thank you for another day of light."

"Beautifully done, sister."

"Thank you, Luna." Celestia smirked without turning around. "I did think that sunrise was particularly smooth."

"'Twas, indeed." Princess Luna stifled

a yawn as she stepped forward to meet her elder sister. The contrast of the rich, velvety darkness of Luna's blue hide next to Celestia's pale, pearly complexion was stark. It mirrored the colours of the skies that they each watched over. Light and dark. Night and day.

But the sisters were not so different. In addition to raising the sun and the moon, they both ruled over Equestria, protecting its inhabitants from harm.

"You seem more exhausted than usual, Luna." Celestia furrowed her brow in concern as her sister yawned again. "Was the night not tranquil?"

"I must confess," Luna offered with a deep exhale, "I am feeling the effects of a night-time most threatened." She pointed her hoof toward the eastern window. "Peril on the coast."

"The coast? Tell me, sister," Celestia urged. "What happened? Is there anything I need to attend to on this day?" Celestia tried to remain calm as she spoke her words. Perhaps it was because she'd had hundreds of moons of experience dealing with crises under her crown, or perhaps she knew that panicking was the quickest way to derail a solution. Deep breaths and a steady voice were the key. Always maintain a calm composure, and those around would follow suit.

Princess Luna shook her head. Her dark, flowing mane billowed around the sides of her face. "It was just a manticore disturbance on the coastline," Luna explained, lifting her hoof toward the east. "Once my presence was known, I was able to reason with them. Until the

Carcinus showed up… *He* came out of nowhere." She raised her brow in mild exasperation. Luna was tough, so this minor display signalled that the disaster was worse than she was saying.

Celestia stiffened. "Carcinus again?" she said with a frown, picturing the beast in her mind. The giant crabs were the size of small buildings and could be quite temperamental. But they were also gentle and understanding. A pony just had to know how to talk to them, to use kindness. "There have been far too many disturbances for my liking as of late. Perhaps I should not go to Monacolt after all. I'll just head to Horseshoe Bay and—"

"Sister, *no*." Luna stepped in to block Celestia's path to the door. Her face grew stern. "You must keep your promise to

Duchess Diamond Waves. You're the only pony who can help her, correct?"

"She seems to believe that the students at her magic school need my help." Celestia bit her lip and reconsidered. It was a struggle for her to relinquish responsibility of Equestria by leaving the capital, but even more of a struggle to let down an old friend in her hour of need. Celestia nodded. "You're right. I must go to her. With any luck, I'll have the students of Monacolt back on track within a few risings of the sun."

Celestia glided toward the balcony again, and Luna soon stood beside her. Both princesses watched over the stirrings of the waking city below in silent reverence. The Canterlot ponies were just beginning to fill the cobblestone paths.

A pair of royal guards in their golden

armour trotted toward the castle, their blue-feathered helmet plumes bobbing up and down as they stepped in time. Across the main plaza, a milk pony was making his morning rounds and placing glass bottles of fresh cream in front of each café and residence. On the other side, a group of young colts and fillies trotted together, giggling and teasing one another. Celestia smiled to herself as she watched them surreptitiously. Her young unicorn students were vivacious – bright as the sun and bursting with talent. What could be so different about the students at Diamond Waves's academy? Celestia wondered. Whatever the reason for their struggle, Princess Celestia was about to find out. She'd be lying if she said she wasn't intrigued by the adventure.

☆ ☆ ☆

Princess Luna raised an eyebrow at Celestia. "Are you really asking me that again?" The blue mare trotted around her sister in a circle, wondering if her sibling would ever learn to trust her. Celestia hardly ever let anypony know when she was worried, but Luna always could tell. And right now, Celestia's golden neckplate jewelry was on slightly crooked. Otherwise, Celestia was the picture of perfection.

"I know I need to start my journey, for it is long, but I just want to be absolutely sure," Celestia replied from the seat of the carriage. A soft pink glow came from her horn. She lifted a saddlebag bearing a picture of her golden sun cutie mark onto the seat next to her. "You're positive you can handle Canterlot on your own? Even with the situation at Horseshoe Bay?"

"I wish you would have more faith in me, Celie."

"I do, it's just that—"

Luna's face grew serious. "All right, you caught me. I'm planning to transform to Nightmare Moon mode as soon as you leave the border!" It was her favourite way to tease Celestia. After Luna had acted up and been banished to the moon, her sister was very touchy about the subject. But the two sisters were past that now. Celestia rolled her eyes, and Luna's face broke into a smirk. "Just teasing you, sister. I know that you worry about me watching over the day, so I've brought in somepony who is very competent to help out at your school and to look over Canterlot while I rest."

"Surprise!" a purple Alicorn with a pink star-shaped cutie mark trotted up to meet them. "Princess Luna said you needed a little bit of assistance."

"Twilight Sparkle!" Celestia exclaimed, embracing the pony. "What a pleasure it is to see you again, my faithful student."

Read
Princess Celestia and
the Royal Rescue
to find out what happens next!

Turn the page for a
special surprise from
Fluttershy!

Dear reader,

With the help of my furry friends, I made these bonus pages just for you! Hum a little tune as you fill them out and then share them with all your special animal friends.

Your Pegasus pal,
Fluttershy

Snuggle Pets

The day is done, and it's time for Princess Celestia to lower the sun. Fluttershy needs to help all her pets find their beds so she can tuck them in for a night of sweet sleep. Can you match the critter with its correct home?

MIGRATION DESTINATIONS

These birds are migrating, a seasonal journey where they fly south to stay warm during winter and then back north for summer. Can you help the birds find their way through the trees and clouds to get to their southern homes? When it's time for the Winter Wrap-Up, the ponies will welcome them back home.

START

FINISH

ANIMAL INSTINCTS

Nopony loves learning about animals more than Fluttershy! Sometimes she even travels to faraway places to study different kinds of creatures, like the Breezies. Are there any animals in your neighbourhood that you like to watch in the wild? Use the space below to record what you see the animals doing. Be sure to keep a safe distance so you don't disturb the creatures.

Type of Animal	Observations
Sparrow	Building a nest in backyard tree, chirping

FEEDING TIME

*One important part of caring for any
pet is making sure it has lots of healthy
food! Angel Bunny loves to nibble on all
kinds of fresh fruits and vegetables, but
his absolute favourite is cherries. Circle
the cherries below to feed Angel his treat!*

The Element of Kindness Diary Entry

Fluttershy is known throughout Ponyville and Equestria for her gentle and caring soul, which is why she represents the Element of Kindness. What was the last kind thing you did for a friend or stranger? Write about it here!

The Top Hat Bunny Cabaret

In the story, Flim and Flam put on a show featuring lots of talented bunnies. Can you remember all the amazing things they could do? Test your memory by filling in the blanks!

1. Juggle _____

2. _____ ___ walls

3. _____ macaroni

4. lift a _____

WHINNYLAND FAIR GAMES 1:
Apple Barrel Challenge

Rarity and Twilight Sparkle have decided to try their hooves at some carnival games at Whinnyland. Can you help them win a stuffed toy by counting the fresh apples in each barrel? Don't include the apples somepony already ate!

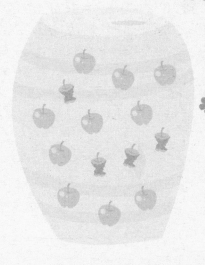

_____

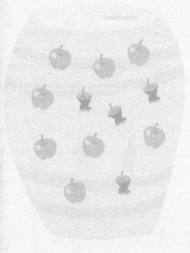

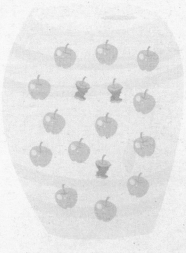

_____   _____

MONARCH MONIKERS

Fluttershy loves all creatures but has a special affinity for butterflies (just like her cutie mark shows)! She's decided to open a butterfly sanctuary and would like to invite some new friends to come and live there. Help her out by giving the butterflies below some beautiful names. Try coloring them in, too!

WHINNYLAND FAIR GAMES 2:
Pinkie Pie's Balloon Darts

Pinkie Pie has asked Fluttershy to play her favourite Whinnyland game with her. Each pony gets three darts to throw at the balloons. If a balloon pops, the pony gets to keep the prize inside. Help Pinkie Pie and Fluttershy by drawing some fun prizes in the balloons! Hint: What might each pony like?

Prized Pets

Fluttershy loves animals more than anything in the whole world. What are some of your favourite creatures? Use the awards stand below to draw your three favourites of all time!

1

2

3

THE CHICKEN DANCE

For Pinkie Pie's performance at the fair, she must make sure she has all her chickens in a row. Look at the chickens below and circle the one that is different—it belongs to another pony!

WHERE HAVE EWE GONE?

Along with her flock of sheep, Fluttershy has lost a few words at the Furry Friends Fair! Can you help her find them? The words may be horizontal, vertical, diagonal, or even backwards!

ANGEL BUNNY   FRIENDS

EWE   HERDING

FAIR   WHINNYLAND

FLUTTERSHY   WINONA

W	H	I	N	N	Y	L	A	N	D	G
T	L	V	Y	Y	W	Z	W	G	H	F
G	E	Q	H	N	N	H	C	K	M	R
N	V	M	S	N	V	E	Q	C	X	I
I	A	W	R	U	J	D	S	X	N	E
D	W	E	E	B	Z	C	T	E	N	N
R	I	B	T	L	V	Q	F	E	S	D
E	N	T	T	E	E	F	W	Y	B	S
H	O	C	U	G	Z	E	Q	N	M	P
M	N	R	L	N	T	R	I	A	F	B
C	A	S	F	A	O	O	X	C	Z	W

ENJOY YOUR FAVOURITE PONY ADVENTURES ON DVD AND DIGITAL HD